Table of Contents

Katie Woo's

Neighborhood

Open Wide, Katie!

by Fran Manushkin

illustrated by Laura Zarrin

PICTURE WINDOW BOOKS
a capstone imprint

Katie Woo's Neighborhood is published by Picture Window Books,
a Capstone imprint
1710 Roe Crest Drive
North Mankato, Minnesota 56003
www.capstonepub.com

Cataloging-in-Publication Data is available on the
LIbrary of Congress website.
ISBN: 978-1-5158-4814-1 (library binding)
ISBN: 978-1-5158-5874-4 (paperback)
ISBN: 978-1-5158-4818-9 (eBook PDF)

Summary: When Katie visits the dentist, the dental hygienist, Ms. Malek,
makes her feel happy and brave.

Graphic Designer: Bobbie Nuytten

Printed and bound in the USA.
PA100

Chapter 1

Fierce Teeth

Katie Woo was at the zoo.

She told her mom, "I love

the alligator. He's so fierce!"

"Look at those teeth," said Katie's dad. "He must need a big toothbrush."

Katie laughed. "For sure!"

"That reminds me," said Katie's mom. "You are seeing the dentist tomorrow. The hygienist will be cleaning your teeth."

"Cool," said Katie. "I love Ms. Malek."

On the way to the dentist, Katie saw Haley O'Hara and her five brothers and sisters. Katie told Haley, "I'm going to see Ms. Malek."

Haley said, "Ms. Malek told us we six kids have lost thirty-five baby teeth."

"Wow!" Katie smiled. "That's a lot of visits from the tooth fairy."

Chapter 2
At the Dentist

Katie and her mom
hurried to the dentist's
office. The waiting room
was a fun place, filled with
books and toys.

Ms. Malek greeted Katie with a big smile. Katie could see that Ms. Malek was a great brusher and flosser.

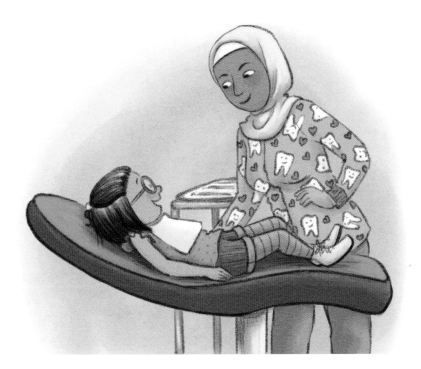

Katie liked taking a ride

in the big blue chair.

"Now, open wide," said

Ms. Malek.

Katie opened wide, like

an alligator.

Ms. Malek used a tiny mirror to look at each of Katie's teeth.

"Looking good!" she said. "I don't see any cavities."

Ms. Malek cleaned Katie's teeth with a cool brush and paste. Katie's smile looked fabulous!

She asked Ms. Malek,

"How do animals clean their

teeth?"

"Well, I know what a

hippo does," said Ms. Malek.

"A hippo opens her mouth and a fish swims in. He eats the food between her teeth."

"Ew!" said Katie.

"I'll say!" said Ms. Malek.

Katie's dentist, Dr. Ali, looked at her teeth too. He told her, "Next time we will take X-rays."

"Cool," said Katie. "I love how weird teeth look on X-rays!"

Katie had fun picking a new
toothbrush.

"I want pink," she decided.

"And cherry toothpaste."

Katie got a toy too.

Chapter 3

Big Smile

On the way home, Katie

saw Pedro and JoJo. Katie told

them about hippos and fish.

"Ew!" said JoJo.

"Gross!" said Pedro.

Pedro told Katie, "The dentist at the zoo has to clean the tiger's teeth."

"Wow!" said Katie.

"He must be brave!"

"The tiger is not awake," said Pedro. "The dentist gives him medicine to make him sleep."

"Good idea!" said Katie.

Before bedtime, Katie

flossed and brushed her

teeth. She smiled at herself

in the mirror.

As Katie's dad tucked her into bed, she said, "When I grow up, maybe I will work at the zoo and clean the elephant's tusks."

"Wow!" said Katie's dad.

"You like to think big."

"I do!" agreed Katie.

She fell asleep with a

big smile.

Glossary

cavities (KAV-uh-tees)—holes or hollow spaces found in teeth

dentist (DEN-tist)—someone who is trained in the care, treatment, and repair of teeth and the fitting of false teeth

fabulous (FAB-yuh-luhss)—wonderful

fierce (FIHRSS)—very strong or extreme

flosser (FLAWSS-er)—a person who regularly uses dental floss, a thin strand of thread used to clean between the teeth

hygienist (hye-JEH-nist)—a person trained to know how to clean and X-ray teeth

medicine (MED-uh-suhn)—a drug or other substance used in treating illness

paste (PAYST)—a soft, creamy mixture

Katie's Questions

1. What traits make a good dental hygienist? Would you like to be a dental hygienist? Why or why not?

2. Imagine you are in charge of cleaning an animal's teeth. Write a paragraph about it.

3. Taking care of your teeth is important. Make a poster that shows different ways to take care of your teeth. Be sure to draw a picture!

4. Do you like to go to the dentist? Why or why not?

5. Teeth have different parts, including enamel, crown, dentin, pulp, root, and gum. Research the parts of a tooth, then draw and label a diagram of a tooth.

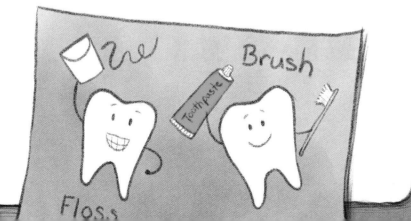

Katie Interviews a Dental Hygienist

Katie: Hi, Ms. Malek! Thanks for telling me all about being a dental hygienist. What do you like best about your job?

Ms. Malek: Since I work at an office that is just for children, I get to meet and help a lot of great kids. I love teaching them how to take care of their teeth.

Katie: I know I love to come see you! You are always fun to talk to.

Ms. Malek: Well, thanks! I like talking to you too, Katie. But not everyone likes coming to see me. Some kids are nervous at the dentist. Then I take extra time to explain everything I'm doing and show them my tools.

Katie: What kind of tools?

Ms. Malek: I have a little mirror that helps me see inside the mouth. I use a metal tool called a scaler to clean the teeth. Then I use a polisher to make the teeth as white and shiny as possible.

Katie: Where did you learn to use all those tools?

Ms. Malek: At college! I have a two-year degree in dental hygiene. To be a hygienist, you also need to have a special license to do the job. We must pass a test to earn that license.

Katie: Do you they teach you to wear fun uniforms at dental hygiene school?

Ms. Malek: Ha! No, I discovered fun uniforms on my own. The shirt I wear is called a smock. I like ones with bright patterns. I also wear gloves, masks, and glasses when I work. They *did* teach me about those things at college!

About the Author

Fran Manushkin is the author of Katie Woo, the highly acclaimed fan-favorite early-reader series, as well as the popular Pedro series. Her other books include *Happy in Our Skin*, *Baby, Come Out!* and the best-selling board books *Big Girl Panties* and *Big Boy Underpants*. There is a real Katie Woo: Fran's great-niece, who doesn't get into trouble like the Katie in the books. Fran lives in New York City, three blocks from Central Park, where she can often be found bird-watching and daydreaming. She writes at her dining room table, without the help of her two naughty cats, Chaim and Goldy.

About the Illustrator

Laura spent her early childhood in the St. Louis, Missouri, area. There she explored creeks, woods, and attic closets, climbed trees, and dug for artifacts in the backyard, all in preparation for her future career as an archeologist. She never became one, however, because she realized she's much happier drawing in the comfort of her own home while watching TV. When she was twelve, her family moved to the Silicon Valley in California, where she still resides with her very logical husband and teen sons, and their illogical dog, Cody.